Shh!
Can you
keep a secret?

You're about to meet the
Ballet Bunnies, who live
hidden at Millie's ballet school.

Are you ready?

Tiptoe this
way . . .

Meet the
Ballet Bunnies

Dolly

You'll never meet
a bunny who
loves to dance as
much as Dolly.

Fifi

If you're in
trouble, Fifi is
always ready to
lend a helping paw!

Pod

Pod loves to build
things out of the
bits and bobs he
finds. He also loves
his tutu!

Trixie

Yawn! When
she's not dancing,
Trixie likes curling
up and having
a nice snooze.

For Yumi

OXFORD
UNIVERSITY PRESS

Great Clarendon Street, Oxford OX2 6DP
Oxford University Press is a department of the University of Oxford.
It furthers the University's objective of excellence in research, scholarship,
and education by publishing worldwide. Oxford is a registered trade mark
of Oxford University Press in the UK and in certain other countries

Database right Oxford University Press (maker)

First published 2020

British Library Cataloguing in Publication Data

Data available

ISBN: 978-0-19277485-9

1 3 5 7 9 10 8 6 4 2

Printed in China

Paper used in the production of this book is a natural,
recyclable product made from wood grown in sustainable forests.
The manufacturing process conforms to the environmental
regulations of the country of origin.

Ballet Bunnies

The New Class

By Swapna Reddy

Illustrated by Binny Talib

OXFORD
UNIVERSITY PRESS

Chapter 1

Millie had been dreaming
of going to Miss Luisa's School of
Dance for months now. So, on her sixth
birthday, when Mum surprised her with
ballet lessons as a gift, she screamed so
loudly with joy that she woke up the
neighbour's elderly dog.

Today was Millie's first lesson.

She spotted a gold sign for her
ballet class and ran her fingers over the
engraved, swirly writing. Unable to stop
the wide grin stretching across her face,
she hurried towards the studio. This
was it. All of Millie's dreams were
about to come true. She pushed
hard on the door.

◦ ✳ ◦

'Watch it!' a voice screeched, as the
wooden door swung open.

A girl in a pink leotard and matching
tutu was sitting on the floor and pulling
on her ballet shoes. She glared at Millie.

'I'm very sorry,' Millie apologized. 'I didn't see you there.'

The girl got to her feet and crossed her arms.

'*You're* in the wrong class,' she said, scowling.

'I don't think so,' Millie said, looking around the room, confused.

'I'm here for ballet too.'

Before either girl could say any more, a teacher called all the children together. 'Come along, Amber,' she said loudly to the girl in pink.

'Yes, Miss Luisa,' Amber replied, her voice now sunny and bright.

Millie followed behind and watched as Amber took a place by the wooden barre

in the middle of the studio. Millie had seen
a barre in the ballet book she'd borrowed
from the library. It helped dancers to
balance whilst they learnt new steps.

Millie copied the others and squeezed
her feet into her ballet slippers, wiggling
her toes. She tapped her sateen feet on the
shiny floor and hopped from foot to foot.

An excited giggle bubbled up from her
tummy as she looked down at her
special shoes.

'Children, we have a new student,'

Miss Luisa said as she
nodded at Millie. 'This
is Millie.'

Millie loved the
way Miss Luisa said
her name. It sounded
like each letter was

dancing to a twinkly melody.

'Hi!' Millie waved at the class,
beaming at each child staring at her.

But no one waved back.

Chapter 2

Miss Luisa nudged Millie
towards the wooden beam, and Millie
joined the line of children.

'First position, everyone,' Miss Luisa
said as she clapped her hands.

First position! Millie had seen this
on a video. Pushing back her shoulders,

Millie stuck out her chin and planted her heels firmly on the floor before pointing her feet outwards.

'Watch Will,' Miss Luisa said, pointing to the boy near Millie. 'He'll show you.'

Millie looked down at her feet and then down at Will's. She couldn't see what she was doing wrong. They *almost* looked the same.

'Come on, Millie,' Miss Luisa said.

The way Miss Luisa said Millie's name was no longer twinkly and melodious but more of an annoyed yell.

Suddenly, the doors to the studio

swung open and in ran a girl with a
rainbow tutu and pink hair.

'I'm sorry I'm late, Miss Luisa,'
the girl yelled as she ran to the barre,
skidding across the floor and sliding to a
stop on her knees.

Millie smiled as she watched the girl clamber to her feet and take a bow.

'Find your place, Samira,' Miss Luisa tutted.

Samira grinned at Millie, but Amber pulled Samira close as soon as she noticed Millie looking their way.

'Now bend into a plié, children,'
Miss Luisa said.

What is a plié? Millie wondered.
Millie watched the children rise
up and down and tried to join in.

'Very nice, Amber,' Miss Luisa
continued. 'Excellent job, Will.'

Millie copied Will and moved up and down in time with him.

'Not quite, Millie,' said Miss Luisa. 'Why don't you start again with first position?'

Millie stopped. Her shoulders sagged forwards as she turned out her feet. She sighed as she saw the others bob up and down without her. The children held their arms high over their heads with their chins pointing out. They all looked like ballet dancers. *Real* ballet dancers.

All apart from Millie.

◦ ✳ ◦

Millie was relieved when the class ended.

She just wanted Mum.

The others disappeared quickly. Soon, she was the last one waiting in the studio.

Millie plonked herself down on the floor and started to rub her sore toes when she thought she heard a tiny voice.

She looked up. There was no one there.

'Hello?' Millie called out.

A tiny shadow darted towards a curtained stage at the end of the studio.

'Hello?' Millie called again.

There was no answer.

Millie got to her feet. She dashed

over to the stage, where she saw the
shadow whizz past again.

'Who's there?' she called out,
grabbing the curtain and yanking it back.
'What is this?' she gasped.

Chapter 3

'Stay still, everyone!
She might not have seen us.'

There, on the stage, amongst a pile
of old ballet slippers and discarded tutus,
were four little bunny rabbits standing as
still as statues.

'How long do we stay still?'

Four TALKING bunnies!

'Just stay still!'

'But I'm stuck in arabesque. I'm not sure how much longer I can hold this.'

'I *can* hear you, you know,' Millie said.

'Oh, bunny fluff!' one of the bunnies sighed. 'You aren't going to scream, are you? Because that's what always happens in the movies.'

'It's true,' another bunny piped up. 'When the humans see something they don't understand in the movies, they scream, and then the thing they don't understand screams back, and then the human screams again, and they both scream because everyone feels terrified.'

'All I feel is a bit hungry for ice cream,' Millie confessed.

The bunnies giggled, their furry bellies jiggling, and Millie found herself chuckling along too.

'I told you she was one of the good ones,' one of the bunnies announced smugly to the others.

Millie reached out her hand, and the tallest of the group jumped on to it.

'Who *are* you?' Millie asked, raising her palm so she and the bunny were nose to nose. '*What* are you?'

'I'm Fifi,' the bunny said, resting
her paws on her hips. 'And we are the
Ballet Bunnies.'

A golden-coloured bunny spun forward in perfect circles and curtsied. 'I'm Dolly.'

The bunny with a tuft of glossy black fur hanging over his eye, stuck out his paw and Millie shook it very gently. 'I'm Pod,' he said.

The tiniest of the bunnies let out a yawn and took Millie's outstretched hand next. 'I'm Trixie,' she said, as Millie tickled her softly under her chin.

Millie climbed up carefully on to

the stage and looked at the piles of ballet shoes that had been stacked and filled with balled-up pom-poms to make a row of beds. Tutus had been laid delicately over the slippers like fluffy bedcovers.

She sat back on her feet. 'I'm Millie, by the way.'

'We know,' Dolly said, hopping up Millie's arm all the way to her shoulder. 'We saw you in class today.'

Dolly spun three perfect pirouettes down Millie's arm.

'How did you do that?' Millie asked, amazed. 'I've tried at home, but I keep falling over.'

Fifi leapt forward and pirouetted alongside Dolly. 'We can show you if you want?'

'Yes, please,' Millie said, watching carefully as Pod joined in.

She stood in a clear spot on the stage as the bunnies talked her through the spin.

'You're doing it, Millie!' Trixie exclaimed.

'I am!' Millie cried back, spinning perfect circles as she tried hard not to lose her focus. She tumbled back on to a pile of leotards, and the bunnies rushed to her. 'I felt like a real dancer!' Millie beamed at Trixie as Fifi, Pod, and Dolly danced a round them.

The sudden creak of the studio door swinging open stopped the bunnies in their tracks.

'Millie?' a voice called loudly.

It was Mum!

Chapter 4

'I have to go!' Millie whispered, jumping up at the sound of her mum's voice.

'Will we see you next week?' Fifi called after her.

Millie hadn't even thought about returning to class. Ballet was difficult—

more difficult than she could've imagined—and she wasn't sure she'd ever make any friends in her class.

But now, as Millie looked at the friendly little rabbits, nestled amongst ballet slippers and tutus, she felt torn.

'There you are!' Mum exclaimed, bustling into the studio.

Millie leapt off the stage, whipping the curtain after her, hoping to shield the little bunnies from her mother.

'Mum!' Millie cried.

'I'm so sorry I'm late, darling,' Mum said, rushing to grab Millie's rucksack. Millie's eyes widened as she spotted

Dolly jumping into the very same rucksack.

'I've got it!' Millie said, diving for the bag before Mum could get it.

◦ ✳ ◦

Millie couldn't concentrate on anything but the little rabbit in her bag.

'Tell me about your class,' Mum said on the walk back down the hill towards home. 'Did you make any friends?'

Millie screwed up her nose. 'Not really,' she said.

'It's still early days,' Mum replied.

Mum chattered away, talking about the time she herself had started dance classes as a child and how she wished she hadn't had to give them up. Millie tried to listen and nodded along, but her tummy fizzed with excitement every time she felt a little nudge from her bag. She wrapped both her hands over a strap and gave it a tiny tug to remind Dolly she was still there.

'Is your bag too heavy?' Mum asked, reaching out a hand.

'No, Mum,' Millie said, releasing her hands. 'It's as light as bunny fluff.'

Dolly sniggered from inside the bag, and Millie had to pretend to cough to cover up the tiny giggle.

Chapter 5

As soon as she and Mum got home, Millie raced upstairs to her room. She delicately laid down her rucksack on her bed, popping open the clasp and opening up the bag.

Dolly hopped out, stretching out her front legs.

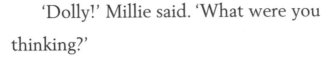

'Dolly!' Millie said. 'What were you thinking?'

'Oh, bunny fluff! I'm really sorry, Millie,' Dolly replied. 'You didn't say whether you were coming to class next week, and I simply had to know.'

She jumped up on to Millie's palm, peering around the bedroom. 'I've left the studio sometimes to see the recitals at the old town theatre, but I've never been in a real bedroom before,' she squealed.

Millie smiled at the little bunny.
'Welcome to my room.'

Dolly squeaked with joy and spun a
perfect pirouette. She sprung around the
room, marvelling at Millie's collection of
ballet books and tutus.
She flipped open a
music box and whirled
in time with the
tiny ballerina
figurine inside.

Millie laughed as Dolly danced amongst her ribbons and held up Millie's hair-bow clips against her silky ears.

'Teatime, Millie,' Mum called up from the kitchen. 'It's noodles—your favourite.'

'I'll be right down,' Millie called back.

'Tea?' Dolly said, raising an eyebrow. She cocked her head to one side. 'Did I hear your mum mention noodles?'

'You want noodles?' Millie asked, confused. 'Do bunnies even eat noodles?'

'This Ballet Bunny does,' Dolly said with a grin.

Chapter 6

'Can I go to my room, Mum?' Millie asked as she scoffed down the last of her noodles and green beans. She hid some for Dolly, too. 'I really want to practise what I learnt today.'

Mum nodded and waved her out of the kitchen.

Millie sprinted up to her bedroom to
find Dolly was no longer dancing around.
Instead, the little bunny was perched by
the mirror and was covered from the tips
of her ears to the bottom of her fluffy tail
in Millie's hair-bow clips.

'What do you think?' Dolly asked. 'Is it too much?'

Millie giggled and removed three bows from Dolly's back and two from her tail. 'That's better,' she said, and Dolly gave a twirl.

Millie found her old tea set. She placed the noodles and beans that she'd snuck into her pockets at dinner into one of the little cups and set it on the floor, alongside a small sugar bowl that she turned upside down as a seat for Dolly.

'Stir-fried noodles,' Dolly said

between mouthfuls. 'They're my favourite.'

'Mine too!' Millie chuckled.

Dolly finished her tea and hopped up on to Millie's bed. She twirled with a length of purple velvet ribbon that hung from the post of the bed until she'd wrapped herself a dress in the soft fabric.

'How does it feel when you dance, Millie?'

Millie sat down, leant against the edge of her bed, and shut her eyes.

'It makes me feel happy,' Millie said. 'And when I jump, I feel like I'm flying through clouds of—'

'Candyfloss?' Dolly finished.

'Yes! That's exactly it,' Millie said. 'Like I'm in a world of candyfloss, light and floaty and—'

'Happy?' Dolly said.

'Exactly!'

'I feel the same way,' Dolly said. She jumped down and landed in Millie's lap. 'And there's no feeling like it.'

Millie and Dolly danced around the
room, practising their pirouettes and
pliés. Dolly helped Millie turn out her
feet just like Miss Luisa had
said to in class.

Before they knew it, Dolly was jumping out of sight as Mum came in to turn out the lights for bedtime.

'I had so much fun dancing with you today,' Millie said, a bit later, as she pulled the bedcovers over Dolly.

'Me too,' Dolly smiled. 'It's just like candyfloss.' She yawned. 'Sharing candyfloss with others is always more fun than getting sticky whiskers all on your own.'

Millie hugged Dolly close, and they both drifted off to a sleep full of pirouettes and the lightest candyfloss.

◦ ✳ ◦

Millie woke the next morning to a fluffy tail in her face and tiny, snoring Dolly stretched out next to her.

'You should get back to the studio,' Millie said, waking the bunny gently. 'The others might be worried.'

Dolly's silky ears bobbed in agreement. 'Are you coming back next week?' Dolly asked.

Millie felt a heavy feeling in her tummy

as she remembered the lesson with Miss
Luisa and Amber and Will. But watching
Dolly reminded Millie of their candyfloss
world, and the heavy feeling started to lift.

Millie nodded. 'I'll be there,' she said.

Dolly smiled, and Millie watched as
she jumped through the open window,
off the window ledge, and on to the

hammock strung up in the garden.

'Will you be OK?' she called after Dolly.

'I'll be fine,' Dolly said. 'It's the same route home as it is from the theatre.'

Millie waved goodbye, and the little bunny hurried off through the gap in the garden gate and back home.

Chapter 7

It had been a week since
Millie had found herself hurrying
through the open doors of Miss Luisa's
School of Dance.

She'd thought of nothing else but the
Ballet Bunnies all week. But now, back
in the studio, she felt further away from

them than ever before. She had to get
through this lesson to see Fifi, Trixie, Pod,
and Dolly again—but as she watched
Will land perfect sautés one after another,
she wondered if she could.

Millie slid on her ballet shoes and joined the others.

'Children, today you will be working in pairs,' Miss Luisa said, tapping the barre. 'Samira, you will work with Will. And Amber, you will work with Millie.'

Millie felt like her stomach dropped right through the floor of the studio.

'But Miss Luisa,' Amber began in her sweetest voice, 'Millie can't even do a basic *first position*. I wouldn't want her to hold me back.'

Millie hung her head. She'd practised all week, remembering all the advice Dolly had given her, but Amber's words made her feel like her feet were glued fast to the ground and her arms were made of lead. She held on tight to the little bunny's words of encouragement.

'I've been practising, Miss Luisa,' Millie found herself saying. She forced

out her feet just like Dolly had shown her and demonstrated a perfect first position.

'Very good, Millie!' Miss Luisa said, raising an eyebrow at Amber.

Before Amber could say anything back, Miss Luisa started the class.

'Face your partner, children,' Miss Luisa said. 'Imagine you are their reflection. Mirror their moves.'

Millie watched Will and Samira. Will flung his arm high and Samira matched it. He lifted his leg and Samira copied. Millie smiled. It was like magic. As though an invisible string connected them.

'You're meant to be facing *me*,' Amber barked at Millie.

Millie took a deep breath and faced Amber.

At the exact same time, Amber threw out her arm over the barre and Millie bent her legs.

'Girls!' Miss Luisa said, shaking her head. 'You need to mirror *each other.*'

'Yes, Miss Luisa,' Amber said, with a bright smile.

She whipped her head round to face Millie. '*You're* meant to be following *me.*'

'Why can't you follow me?' Millie asked.

'Because you don't know anything about ballet,' Amber retorted.

Amber strode back from Millie and jumped up into a sauté.

'Come on then,' Amber said, meanly.

Both Amber and Millie prepared
to sauté. But as they took off, Amber
switched the move to a *saut de basque*,
spinning into a pirouette in the air.
Millie mirrored Amber, but her legs

locked around each other and she crashed
to the floor, knocking against the barre.

'Millie!' Miss Luisa cried.
'Concentrate, please.'

Amber sniggered and got ready to
jump again, but Millie didn't bother to

copy her this time. Will laughed along with Amber as Millie clambered to her feet. Tears streamed down her face and she ran across the studio to the toilets, as far away from the ballet class as she could get.

Chapter 8

'Millie?'

Dolly, Trixie, Fifi, and Pod hopped across the floor of the girls' toilets, following the sounds of sobs.

'I won't go back,' Millie cried.
'I won't.'

The four bunnies crawled under the door of the furthest cubicle, where they found Millie on the floor, hugging her knees as she cried.

'Oh, Millie,' Fifi said. 'That Amber was rotten to you.'

Dolly hopped up over Millie's foot and landed on her knees. She nuzzled her way under Millie's downturned head and squished her face into Millie's, gently

licking away her tears.

Millie dropped her chin down to her chest. 'I'm just not good enough.'

'Bunny fluff,' Fifi dismissed. 'Yes you are.'

'I can't keep up with the others,' Millie said, her voice small.

Dolly jumped into Millie's hand. 'But you don't have to, Millie. It's OK to go at your own pace,' she said gently.

'This is just your second lesson,' Pod agreed. 'Amber has been coming here since she was tiny—'

'Maybe even tinier than me,' Trixie piped up, getting a giggle out of Millie.

'It's true,' Dolly said with a kind smile. 'You'll be dancing like the others with more lessons. Remember why you love dancing. Remember the candyfloss.'

Millie wiped away the tears on her face. She'd made up her mind.

'You're right,' she sniffed. 'I *do* love dancing. But I would rather just carry on dancing at home.' Millie wrapped her arms around herself. 'That way I don't have to deal with the all the bad bits, like Amber.'

The bunnies looked at one another, their shoulders slumped and their wide eyes shiny with tears.

'We will miss you so much, Millie!'
Fifi cried, as Dolly ran off out of the
bathroom.

'And I'll miss you too,' Millie said,
her chest aching as though her heart was
being pulled in half.

She scooped up Fifi, Pod, and Trixie.
Her chest aching, she kissed each of them

gently on the head and held them close.

'Where's Dolly?' Millie asked, looking
for the fourth bunny. 'I can't go without

saying goodbye to her. I just can't!'

Fifi, Pod, and Trixie hurried down, searching under the cubicle doors for Dolly.

'Dolly?' Fifi called out.

'I'm here,' Dolly said, reappearing in the room.

'Oh, Dolly!' Millie cried. 'I'm so glad you came back.'

Dolly hopped over to Millie's open palm and nuzzled it reassuringly. She then carefully placed a tiny object into Millie's hand.

Millie peered at her palm. 'What's this, Dolly?'

'It's for you,' the bunny replied.
'I want you to have something
to remember us by.'

Millie picked up the tiny object. It was a strip of a soft pink tutu, rolled up and fastened at one end with one of Millie's hair clips.

'It's candyfloss!' Millie said, hugging the bunny close.

Millie took the little clip. She looked in the mirror before sliding it into her hair. As she touched the rosy fabric, she gazed down at the bunnies,

remembering how they had pirouetted
together on the stage when they had first
met and how much fun they'd had.

Chapter 9

The bathroom door rattled, and the bunnies jumped out of sight.

Millie turned to see Samira come into the toilets and then smile kindly at her.

'I thought what Amber did today was really unfair,' Samira said.

Millie looked down, unable to meet Samira's gaze.

Samira squatted down to look up at Millie. 'She can be a bit mean sometimes,' she said softly.

'It doesn't matter,' Millie said, sticking out her chin. 'I'm not sure I'm coming back here again anyway.'

'Really?' Samira questioned.

Millie shook her head. 'You're all way ahead of me.'

'Yeah, because we've been here for aaaages,' Samira said, pulling Millie to stand next to her. 'This is your second lesson, and I saw your first position was looking really good.'

Millie felt a warm feeling in her chest. 'I've been working on that all week.'

'It really shows,' Samira encouraged her.

Samira stuck out her feet into first position. Out of the corner of her eye, Millie spotted Dolly hiding behind the bin. Dolly stuck her feet into first position, too, and nodded to Millie to do the same.

Then Samira switched to second position, and Millie followed.

'Miss Luisa would love your posture,' Samira said. 'She's always telling me to straighten my neck like a giraffe.' She relaxed her feet and stretched her neck forward. 'Do I look like a giraffe, Millie?'

Millie chuckled. 'You're the best giraffe I've ever met in the toilets.'

The girls straightened out their necks and walked around the bathroom, each doing their best impressions of a giraffe. When Samira tried to pirouette as a giraffe, she knocked into Millie, and the two tumbled to the floor in a giggling

heap. Dolly was right. Dancing with others was definitely more fun than dancing on your own.

'I wish you weren't leaving,' Samira said to Millie. 'I was going to ask if we could be partners next time.'

Millie sat up and stared at Samira. 'You wanted *me* to be *your* partner?' she said, astounded.

'If you don't mind,' Samira said, squeezing in closer to Millie and giving her a friendly nudge.

'I'd love that!' Millie grinned, nudging her new friend back.

'I love your hair clip,' Samira said, tilting her head to admire the tiny pin. 'It looks like a ball of candyfloss! I love candyfloss.'

'Me too,' said Millie.

'I especially like dressing up as candyfloss,' Samira said.

Millie giggled as Samira pretended to nibble her fluffy tutu.

'I hope you don't leave, Millie,' Samira said. She stood up and hopscotched to the bathroom door and back towards the studio.

Millie watched the door swing shut, and the bunnies scrambled out of their hiding places.

What Dolly had said stuck in Millie's mind. Maybe it didn't matter that she wasn't quite as good as the other dancers. Maybe all that mattered in the end was that it was more fun to enjoy candyfloss with others.

'I don't want you to leave, Millie,' Dolly pleaded, looking up at Millie. 'Please say you'll come back.'

Dancing like a giraffe with Samira had filled Millie's tummy with that warm, happy feeling of flying through clouds of candyfloss—the feeling that Millie only ever got from dancing. Now that she and Samira could be partners,

Millie couldn't help but feel every week
could be a candyfloss week.

She took a breath. 'You know what?'
Millie said, beaming at the bunnies.
'I think I will.'

'Sticky whiskers for everyone!'
Fifi cheered as Millie scooped up
the Ballet Bunnies into the hugest,
fluffiest hug.

Basic ballet moves

First position

Second position

Third
position

Fourth
position

Fifth position

About the author

Award-winning author
Swapna Reddy, who also
writes as Swapna Haddow,
lives in New Zealand with
her husband and son and
their dog, Archie.

If she wasn't writing
books, she would love
to run a detective agency
or wash windows because
she's very nosy.

About the illustrator

Binny Talib is a Sydney based illustrator who loves to create wallpaper, branding, children's books, editorial, packaging and anything else she can draw all over.

Binny recently returned from living in awesome Hong Kong and now works happily on beautiful Sydney harbour with other lovely creative folks, drinking copious amounts of dandelion tea, and is inspired by Jasper her rescue cat.

If you enjoyed this adventure, you might also like . . .